PINOCCHIO

Original story by Carlo Collodi
Retold by Claire O'Brien
Series Advisor Professor Kimberley Reynolds
Illustrated by Victor Rivas

OXFORD
UNIVERSITY PRESS

Letter from the Author

My favourite sound is
children giggling, so I decided
a long time ago to become a
writer of funny stories. Writers
can make children giggle without
ever having to stop and be
sensible, so it's the perfect job for
me! I have a grown-up son and
husband who both have big, bushy beards. I like
snoozing in the shade, growing vegetables and
riding my bicycle.

Pinocchio was great fun to write because so
many crazy things happen to that little puppet!
For me, this story is about finding the courage
to change our attitude, which can be very
difficult. When we learn to help others like
Pinocchio does, our problems begin to disappear
and we become happier every day. That was true
when this story was written, over one hundred
and thirty years ago, and it is still true today.

Claire O'Brien

Chapter One

There was once an old man called Geppetto. He was very poor and he had no wife or children, so he sometimes felt lonely.

One day, Geppetto found a log of cherry wood while he was out walking.

Cherry wood is too good to burn on the fire, he thought. *I think I'll carve it into a puppet.*

As he carved the puppet's head, Geppetto decided to call it Pinocchio, because that was the name of the happiest man he had ever known.

It will be a boy, Geppetto thought, *and I will care for him as if he were my son, then I won't feel so lonely.*

As soon as Geppetto had completed the puppet, he put it down on the table. To Geppetto's astonishment, the wooden boy sprang up at once, and sprinted around the room.

'How wonderful!' Geppetto said to the puppet. 'You will be able to go to school with the other boys.'

The puppet stuck his tongue out at Geppetto. 'I don't want to go to school,' he said. 'I just want to play.'

'You can't play all the time, my dear little Pinocchio,' said Geppetto. 'Now, you must eat something. How about a nice pear?'

Pinocchio didn't eat just one pear; he guzzled all three that were on the table. Kind old Geppetto didn't scold him because he was delighted to have a son, even a wooden one.

'Goodness!' he said. 'You have a healthy appetite. You will soon grow big and strong and be able to work.'

'I don't want to work,' said Pinocchio. 'Not ever. I just want to have fun.'

Geppetto laughed. 'Everyone has to work,' he said. 'But right now, it's time for bed.'

'I don't want to go to bed,' said Pinocchio, and he leaped around the room, sticking his tongue out at his father for another half an hour before poor, exhausted Geppetto finally persuaded him to go to sleep.

'You're a little bit naughty,' Geppetto whispered, as Pinocchio slept, 'but I love you very much.'

In the morning, Geppetto dressed the puppet smartly and said, 'Now you are ready for school.'

'I cannot go to school,' Pinocchio grumbled, 'because I don't have a spelling book.'

Geppetto went out into the snow and sold his old coat to buy Pinocchio a spelling book. On the way home he went into the baker's shop to buy the boy a big bread roll to take for his lunch.

The puppet still complained. 'Do I have to go to school?' he moaned.

'Yes, of course,' Geppetto insisted. 'You don't want to grow up silly, do you?'

So Pinocchio set off for school, and he might have got there if he hadn't heard loud music playing.

The baker was standing outside his shop.

'What's happening?' Pinocchio asked him.

'The puppet theatre is here,' said the baker.

'Come and see the puppet show!' cried the puppet master, who was called Fire-Eater. 'It's only five pennies.'

Pinocchio didn't have even one penny, but he had an idea.

'Would you like to buy this spelling book?' he asked the baker. 'It hasn't been used and it must have cost at least ten pennies, but you can have it for the excellent price of just five.'

The baker scratched his beard. 'Well,' he said, 'my daughter does need a new spelling book. Let me look at it.'

He checked inside the spelling book and scratched his beard again.

'Very well,' he said at last. 'It's a deal.'

And they shook hands.

As Pinocchio waited outside the theatre with his five shiny pennies, he ate the bread roll that he should have saved for his lunch. Just as he finished the last mouthful, a grasshopper jumped onto a wall nearby and warned him, 'If you don't go to school, Pinocchio, you'll grow up really silly. You'll be a complete donkey.'

'Go away you horrid insect,' said Pinocchio. 'I don't want to go to school. I want to see the puppets.'

'What about poor Geppetto?' the grasshopper asked. 'He sold his coat so that you could go to school with a spelling book and with that bread roll that you have just gobbled up, and now he's shivering with cold as he works hard to earn enough money for your supper.'

'Oh shut up you bossy bug!' Pinocchio shouted, and he threw a heavy stone at the grasshopper and squashed him FLAT.

Oh dear, thought Pinocchio. *I didn't mean to do that.*

But it was too late. The grasshopper was dead and the puppet show was starting.

Chapter Two

Pinocchio cheered and laughed at the puppets, but Fire-Eater the puppet master was watching him.

I'll have that wooden boy for my theatre, he thought. *I'll make him dance and sing.*

When the show finished he grabbed Pinocchio and kidnapped him.

'You will work for me,' he snarled, 'or I will use you as firewood to cook my supper.'

Pinocchio looked at the blazing fire. He looked at the other puppets, who were trembling with fear. Then he looked at Fire-Eater's gigantic hands and his whip and his long, long beard that dragged on the floor. Oh, how Pinocchio wished he had gone to school that morning! But it was too late.

'Show this boy how we burn puppets!' Fire-Eater ordered his assistants.

They grabbed Harlequin, who was Pinocchio's favourite puppet, and dragged him towards the fire. Pinocchio fell on his knees in front of Fire-Eater.

'Please don't burn Harlequin,' he begged. 'He's a much finer puppet than I am. He can dance and sing and turn somersaults. Don't burn him, burn me instead.'

This touched Fire-Eater's heart, because even monsters have hearts. When his heart was touched by kindness, Fire-Eater sneezed. He sneezed explosively.

ACHOOO, ACHOOO, ACHOOO!

'Let Harlequin go,' Fire-Eater commanded, when he had finished sneezing. 'Go home to your father,' he told Pinocchio. 'Take this money to him.'

He gave Pinocchio five gold coins. The boy thanked him and left as quickly as he could.

I will buy my father a new coat with jewels for buttons, Pinocchio thought as he hurried home. *And I will never miss school again.*

He would have been such a good boy if only he hadn't met a fox with a wooden leg and a cat who was blind.

Chapter Three

The fox and the cat bowed and wished Pinocchio good evening. The foolish puppet told them about his adventure, and about the five gold coins.

The fox asked, 'Would you like to make your five gold coins into five hundred or five thousand?'

Pinocchio gasped. 'Of course!' he said.

The cat purred. The fox licked his lips.

'All you have to do,' said the cat, 'is go to the Field of Miracles.'

'Is it very far?' asked Pinocchio. 'Because I should be getting home. My father will be fretting.'

'It's just beyond the forest,' said the cat. 'But you must go at night, or the magic won't work.'

Pinocchio shook his head. 'I shouldn't stay out that late.'

The fox and the cat shrugged and started to walk away.

'Wait!' called Pinocchio. 'How is it possible to turn five pieces of gold into five hundred or five thousand?'

'Simple,' said the cat. 'Plant them in the ground in the Field of Miracles and they will grow into a bush full of gold coins. Imagine that!'

Pinocchio sighed. *Just imagine!* he thought. *I would never have to work or go to school.*

'All right,' the foolish boy agreed. 'Show me the way.'

The cat and the fox told Pinocchio the way to the Field of Miracles and he set off through the forest.

Deep inside, he sat down to wait until dark. A shimmering shape appeared in front of him.

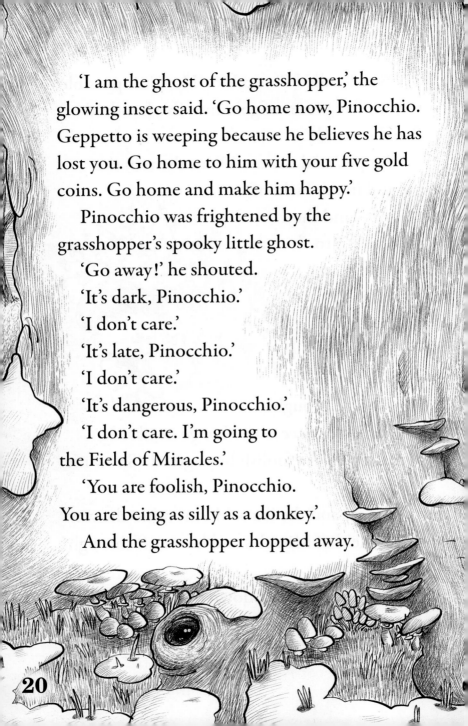

'I am the ghost of the grasshopper,' the glowing insect said. 'Go home now, Pinocchio. Geppetto is weeping because he believes he has lost you. Go home to him with your five gold coins. Go home and make him happy.'

Pinocchio was frightened by the grasshopper's spooky little ghost.

'Go away!' he shouted.

'It's dark, Pinocchio.'

'I don't care.'

'It's late, Pinocchio.'

'I don't care.'

'It's dangerous, Pinocchio.'

'I don't care. I'm going to the Field of Miracles.'

'You are foolish, Pinocchio. You are being as silly as a donkey.'

And the grasshopper hopped away.

Chapter Four

At that very moment, two bandits jumped out of the bushes shouting, 'Your money or your life!'

They wore big black sacks with eye holes and carried sharp knives. Pinocchio ran as fast as he could. As he ran he heard the bandits getting closer.

'We'll get you, we'll get you!' they roared.

Pinocchio hid the coins under his tongue and shut his mouth tightly. He leaped over a hedge and ran across fields; he waded along a muddy ditch and then climbed a tall tree, but the bandits spotted him. They set fire to the tree and poor Pinocchio had to jump to the ground or be sizzled up. The bandits grabbed him.

'The money is in your mouth. Open up!' said the first bandit, who had a long red tail peeping out from under his sack, rather like a fox.

They rattled him
this way and that,
and shouted at him.
Then they rattled
him again until his
mouth fell open and
out dropped the five
gold coins.

Then the bandits
tied poor Pinocchio
to a tree.

'You will soon
freeze to death out
here,' said the second
bandit, who had
fluffy paws, rather
like a cat.

And the pair of
them ran off into
the dark.

Chapter Five

Not far away, in a tall white house, a
blue-haired fairy was watching from her
balcony. A falcon perched beside her. The fairy
pointed to Pinocchio and whispered to the bird,
'Use your strong beak to cut the ropes that tie
that wooden boy.'

The falcon flew off and soon
returned, his job done.

'The boy has a fever,' the
falcon told the fairy. 'He
cannot stand up.'

The blue-haired fairy
clapped her hands and
called, 'Coachman!'

Immediately, a tall
poodle appeared, dressed
in smart red velvet.

'Be quick!' said the fairy.
'Bring that wooden boy here!'

The poodle drove his coach into the woods. It was made of whipped cream and biscuits and was full of soft feather cushions. Pulling it along were a hundred pairs of white mice.

Pinocchio felt himself being lifted up. He heard the wheels of the coach turning and felt the softness of the cushions.

When they reached the fairy's house, the coachman carried Pinocchio to a comfortable bed.

The wooden boy felt the soft mattress but he could not open his eyes. He could only whisper, 'Thank you for rescuing me.'

Pinocchio's heart was miserable and his body was exhausted. He missed Geppetto, and how he wished that he had gone straight home.

27

The best doctors in the land had been summoned. They just happened to be a grasshopper's ghost, a crow and an owl.

'Is he alive?' asked the blue-haired fairy, looking worried.

The owl coughed and replied, 'He is either alive or dead, that's certain.'

'No, no,' said the crow. 'He is either dead or alive, that's for sure.'

'Alive or dead,' said the grasshopper's ghost, 'that boy is a fool. He is as silly as a donkey and

he has broken his poor father's heart.'

Pinocchio began to cry.

'It is a fact,' said the owl, 'that when a dead person cries, he is probably alive.'

'No, no,' said the crow. 'It is a fact that when a living person cries, he is probably not dead.'

'Alive or dead,' said the grasshopper's ghost, 'he has a fever and needs medicine.'

The blue-haired fairy brought medicine
and poured some onto a big spoon. Pinocchio
slowly sat up in bed, but the medicine
smelled bitter.

'I'm very grateful for being rescued,' he said,
'but I don't want to take that horrid medicine.'

'You'll be sorry,' said the fairy.

Pinocchio began to cry again. 'I don't care,'
he sobbed.

'Your fever is very bad,'
said the fairy.

'I don't care!'

'You could be dead very
soon,' said the fairy.

'I don't care!'

At that moment the door opened and four black rabbits came into the room. They wore black cloaks with black hoods and they carried a boy-sized coffin on their shoulders.

Pinocchio gasped. 'Who are you?' he asked, trembling.

'We are the Rabbits of Doom,' said the first rabbit, 'and you just said that you don't care if you die, so we've come to take you away.'

'But I'm not dead,' said Pinocchio.

'You soon will be,' said the second rabbit.

'If you don't take your medicine,' said the third.

'You've got about five minutes left,' said the fourth rabbit, checking his pocket watch.

'Oh! Fairy, Fairy!' Pinocchio cried. 'Give me the medicine at once.' And he took the medicine in one big gulp.

The rabbits sighed and shrugged their shoulders.

'That was pointless,' said the first rabbit as they turned and started to leave.

'Yes, a complete waste of time,' said the second.

'We could have collected plenty of other boys tonight,' said the third.

'Plenty of properly dead ones,' said the fourth.

The fairy said nothing. She closed the door behind the rabbits and looked at Pinocchio.

'Now, tell me truthfully,' she said. 'Did you sell your spelling book so that you could go to the puppet show?'

Pinocchio shook his head. 'No,' he said, and as soon as he'd said it, his nose grew longer.

'Oh!' cried Pinocchio, touching his big, wooden nose.

The fairy smiled and asked, 'Did you listen to the cat and the fox instead of going straight home?'

Pinocchio shook his head again. 'No,' he said, and his nose grew so long that it touched the wall.

'Oh, oh! What's happening?' he cried.

The fairy laughed gently. 'You're telling lies, Pinocchio. That's why your nose is growing.'

'I'm sorry,' he said. 'I really am. Please put my nose back how it was.'

The fairy was really
very kind, so she
clapped her hands
and in through
the window
flew a flock of
woodpeckers.
They got
to work
and pecked
Pinocchio's nose
back to the right
size. It didn't
hurt, of course,
because it was
made of wood.

'I'll never tell
another lie. Not ever,'
Pinocchio promised.
And he never did, so his nose
always stayed just the right size.

As soon as Pinocchio's nose was fixed, a giant pigeon flew in. 'Is there a puppet here called Pinocchio?' the bird asked.

'Yes, that's me,' said Pinocchio, feeling his nose.

'I have news about your father,' said the pigeon.

Pinocchio thought of Geppetto and wanted to go home. 'What's happened?' he asked. 'Please tell me he's safe and well.'

The pigeon frowned. 'Your father has set sail in a little boat to search for you. The sea is

stormy and he cannot swim, so he will almost
certainly drown.'

Pinocchio jumped up. 'How can I get to
him?' he asked. 'I must help him.'

'Climb onto my back and hold tightly,' the
pigeon told the boy.

Pinocchio thanked the fairy for her help,
then clambered onto the pigeon's wide, downy
back. The pigeon spread his wings and they
were soon soaring above the clouds, so fast and
so high that Pinocchio didn't dare look down.

When they reached the coast Pinocchio
ran straight to the edge of the water. A dog ran
after him, barking and jumping. The boy could
see Geppetto in his tiny boat, surrounded by
crashing waves.

'Father! Father!' Pinocchio shouted, waving
his arms.

But a huge wave smashed over the boat and
Geppetto vanished ...

'I will save my father!' Pinocchio called, and he jumped into the water. The dog jumped in after him but the silly creature couldn't swim.

'Help me, Pinocchio. Help me!' called the dog, as it coughed and struggled.

'I don't have time,' Pinocchio cried back. 'I have to save my father.'

But he felt sorry for the foolish dog. He couldn't leave it to drown, so he grabbed its tail and dragged the animal back to the beach, before jumping into the waves again.

'Thank you, Pinocchio!' the dog barked
from the shore. 'I won't forget your kindness.'
    Pinocchio swam into the storm. He could
float, being made of wood, but the waves
were so strong that the brave little puppet was
pulled down under the crashing sea.

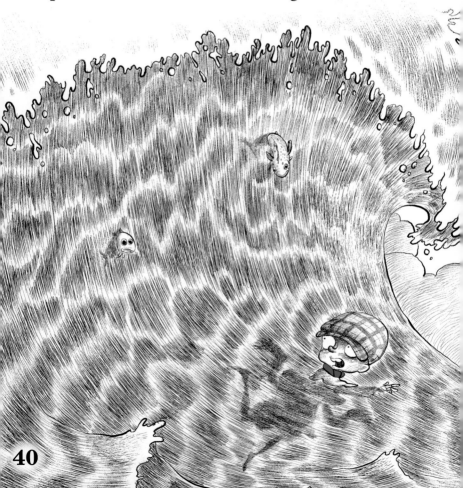

Chapter Six

Pinocchio was washed up the next morning on a sunny beach on the Island of Busy Bees. He dried his tattered clothes and then started walking, feeling very sad about Geppetto, and very hungry.

I will have to beg for food, he thought.

He came to a village where everyone was working. A man went past pushing a cart full of coal. He looked hot and tired.

'Please give me a penny to buy bread and water,' Pinocchio begged.

'I will if you'll help me push this cart,' replied the man.

Pinocchio shook his head. 'That looks like hard work,' he said.

'Then you can stay hungry and thirsty,' said the man, and he walked on.

Next, a man carrying bricks went past.

'Will you give me a penny to buy some bread and water?' Pinocchio pleaded.

'If you help me carry these bricks I'll give you five pennies,' said the man.

Pinocchio shook his head again. 'They look very heavy,' he said.

'Then you can stay hungry and thirsty,' said the man, and he walked on too.

This continued until twenty people had offered Pinocchio some work and he had refused them all.

'I don't want to work. I'm not a donkey,' Pinocchio said to himself.

As he walked through the village a group of children began to follow him and tease him.

'You're made of wood,' one of them shouted. 'You're just a stick puppet!'

'Look at your scruffy clothes,' another one called. 'You look like a big mess!'

They started to chase Pinocchio and pelt him with stones, so the poor, tired, hungry puppet had to run. He fled back to the beach.

'Stick boy! Scruffy stick boy!' they shouted. 'Throw the stick into the sea!'

And the children began to grab him and push him. Pinocchio wasn't strong enough to stop them. They swung him and flung him, and back into the sea he went with a *splash*!

Too tired to swim, Pinocchio drifted on the water until he was scooped up into a giant fishing net. He was squashed between hundreds of wriggling fish and hauled up onto the shoulder of a sea ogre, who carried the net to his cave. The ogre opened the net and began to fry the fish in a giant pan of sizzling oil.

'What's this?' he growled, picking Pinocchio up by his foot and dangling him about. 'This isn't a sardine or a haddock or a salmon.'

'I'm a puppet!' shouted Pinocchio, trying to wriggle free.

'A puppet fish, eh?' said the ogre. 'I've never eaten one of those before. You don't look very tasty but I'll give you a try.'

And he dipped Pinocchio into his dish of flour, covering him from head to toe, *flip flop flip*.

'Please don't eat me!' Pinocchio begged.

Just as the sea ogre was about to throw him into the hot oil a dog ran into the cave, growling and barking. It was the dog that Pinocchio had rescued. The animal jumped up, grabbed the floury puppet in his mouth and ran back to the beach, where he dropped Pinocchio onto the soft sand.

'Thank you for saving me,' said Pinocchio.

'I said I wouldn't forget you,' called the dog, and he ran off barking and wagging his tail.

Chapter Seven

Poor, exhausted Pinocchio set off towards home. It soon began to get dark, but he would have reached his village safely if he hadn't met a boy called Lampwick.

'I have to get back home and get ready for school,' Pinocchio told him. 'Can you tell me the way?'

Lampwick shook his head, saying, 'I'm going somewhere where there aren't any schools. You can play all day and you never have to work.'

'Really?' asked Pinocchio. 'Is there such a place?'

'Yes,' said Lampwick. 'It's called Playland.'

At that moment a cart pulled by twenty-four donkeys stopped beside them. The cart was crammed with excited children.

'You can come, too,' said Lampwick.

Pinocchio shook his head. 'I'm going to be sensible,' he said.

'But there are free sweets in Playland and every day is like a party,' the boy told him.

Pinocchio tried to be strong. 'No, I won't come, thank you,' he said.

'There are no books, no homework and no bossy teachers in Playland,' Lampwick told him, climbing onto the cart.

The wheels started turning.

'It does sound lovely,' said Pinocchio, 'and I really don't want to work.'

'Jump aboard,' called the coachman, 'if you're coming.'

'I suppose I could come for just a little while,' said Pinocchio.

'Come on!' the children cried as the cart moved faster.

'Okay, wait for me!' shouted Pinocchio, and he leaped onto the back of the cart. The coachman cracked his whip and away they went.

Playland was wonderful. There were sweets and a fairground and lots of new friends to play with. That night, Pinocchio slept in a room full of toys and thought he had never been happier.

When he woke up his head was itchy. He scratched it and it felt furry so he looked in the mirror.

'Oh no!' he gasped. 'I've got donkey ears.'

Then his back started to itch. He scratched and scratched and suddenly a long donkey tail burst out through his shorts.

'Oh!' cried Pinocchio, and ran to find Lampwick.

His friend also had donkey ears. He had a donkey tail, too. The boys laughed at each other but all that came out was, 'HEEE AWW, HEEE AWW.'

They looked down and saw that they had donkey hooves and donkey legs. That's when they stopped laughing and felt frightened, and in two more minutes they were no longer boys but little furry donkeys.

The coachman came in and clapped his hands. 'Right, off to market we go,' he said, and led the donkey boys away.

Pinocchio was sold to a cruel circus master who made him dance and spin and jump through hoops. If he made mistakes, he was beaten with a stick. Pinocchio had never been so miserable.

For many weeks, Pinocchio had to dance and jump in front of a crowd. They cheered and roared with laughter and shouted, 'Higher! Jump higher, little donkey.'

So the circus master forced him to jump higher and higher until one day Pinocchio fell and injured his leg.

'You're no good to me now,' said the cruel circus master. 'I shall kill you and make you into a furry carpet to warm my feet,' and he dragged Pinocchio to the top of a cliff and pushed him off.

Poor Pinocchio *splashed* into the sea and sank. But as he sank he turned back into a puppet and began to float up to the surface again.

The puppet boy swam towards a rock, but before he could reach it a huge shark glided by with its enormous jaws gaping open. Pinocchio was sucked right down inside its gigantic belly.

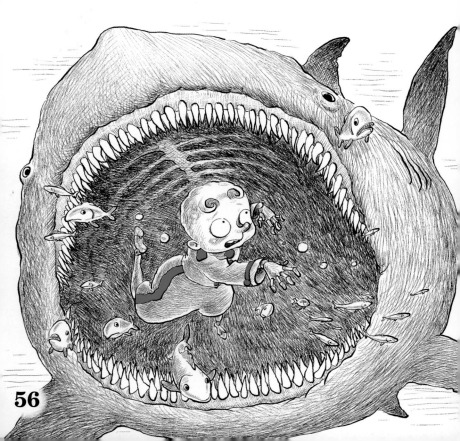

Chapter Eight

It was very dark inside that belly. Pinocchio walked towards a tiny speck of light in the distance. Imagine how amazed he was to find that the light was a candle on a table, and sitting at the table was Geppetto.

They hugged each other and cried with joy.

'Can that really be my dear Pinocchio?'
said Geppetto.

'Yes, Father, and I will never leave you
again,' Pinocchio promised.

'This is the last candle and there is nothing
to eat here,' said Geppetto, sadly. 'I have lived
on cheese and raisins from a ship that the
shark swallowed, but they are all finished now.'

'I will get us to safety,' said Pinocchio.

'But I can't swim,' said Geppetto.

'I will take care of you,' Pinocchio promised.
Slowly and carefully they climbed back
towards the shark's mouth,
tiptoeing over smelly bones
and chewed seaweed.
A helpful tuna fish
led the way. As they
stepped along the
shark's big, floppy
tongue the tuna fish
pointed ahead.

'Look,' she said. 'You can see the stars.'

Pinocchio and Geppetto stared at the sky.

'That's because this shark always sleeps with his big mouth open,' the tuna explained, 'and he snores!'

'Quickly! Climb on my back, Father,' said Pinocchio.

The old man climbed up and brave Pinocchio jumped into the sea. The tuna fish jumped too, and waved them goodbye.

Chapter Nine

After a long, gruelling swim they reached the shore. They walked and walked until they came to a cottage where a gardener lived. By this time Geppetto was very weak.

'Please could you give me some milk for my father?' Pinocchio asked the gardener.

'If you work the pump and bring up one hundred buckets of water for my garden, I will give you some milk,' the man replied.

This time Pinocchio didn't complain. He got to work straight away. It was very hard and took a long time but at the end of the day the gardener paid Pinocchio and gave him some milk.

'You may stay here until your father is well again,' the gardener told Pinocchio, 'if you will work hard every day.'

Pinocchio agreed happily, and thanked the gardener.

Every day, Pinocchio worked for the gardener and cared for his father, who slowly grew stronger again. Even in his spare time the boy didn't rest. He learned how to weave baskets, which he sold at the market to buy everything they needed.

One night, after many months of hard work, Pinocchio had a dream. In the dream the grasshopper and the blue-haired fairy visited him.

'I forgive you for squashing me flat,' said the grasshopper, smiling.

The blue-haired fairy kissed his forehead. 'You have changed,' she told him. 'You have worked hard and cared for Geppetto, like a real son would. Tomorrow you will be rewarded.'

In the morning, there were fine new clothes waiting for Pinocchio, and in the pocket of the jacket there were forty gold coins.

But most wonderful of all, when he looked in the mirror, Pinocchio saw that he was no longer made of wood but of flesh and blood.

'Father! Father!' he shouted. 'Look at me!' and he ran to find Geppetto, who was fully recovered now and was cooking a big breakfast.

Together they danced around the little cottage until they were out of breath, then Pinocchio asked, 'Please, Father, may I go to school today?'

'Of course,' Geppetto agreed. 'And I promise that you will also have plenty of time to play.'